Hank the Pet Sitter

#6

Pete the Very Chatty Parrot

by Claudia Harrington   illustrated by Anoosha Syed

Calico Kid

An Imprint of Magic Wagon
abdopublishing.com

To Lee Wind, transcriptionist extraordinaire and my Friend. —CH

To my family —AS

abdopublishing.com

Printed in the United States of America, North Mankato, Minnesota.
052018
092018

THIS BOOK CONTAINS
RECYCLED MATERIALS

Written by Claudia Harrington
Illustrated by Anoosha Syed
Edited by Tamara L. Britton
Art Directed by Candice Keimig

Library of Congress Control Number: 2018931803

Publisher's Cataloging-in-Publication Data

Names: Harrington, Claudia, author. | Syed, Anoosha, illustrator.
Title: Pete the very chatty parrot / by Claudia Harrington; illustrated by Anoosha Syed.
Description: Minneapolis, Minnesota : Magic Wagon, 2019. | Series: Hank the pet sitter set 2; Book 6
Summary: If Pete the parrot didn't belong to Janie, he would have been the perfect pirate pet! Except for the poop. Everywhere. Hank wants to teach Pete how to talk like a pirate while Janie's gone. But will he be too busy swabbing the decks?
Identifiers: ISBN 9781532131745 (lib.bdg.) | ISBN 9781532132148 (ebook) | ISBN 9781532132346 (Read-to-me ebook)
Subjects: LCSH: Parrots--Juvenile fiction. | Talking birds--Juvenile fiction. | Pet sitting--Juvenile fiction. | Pets--Juvenile fiction.
Classification: DDC [E]--dc23

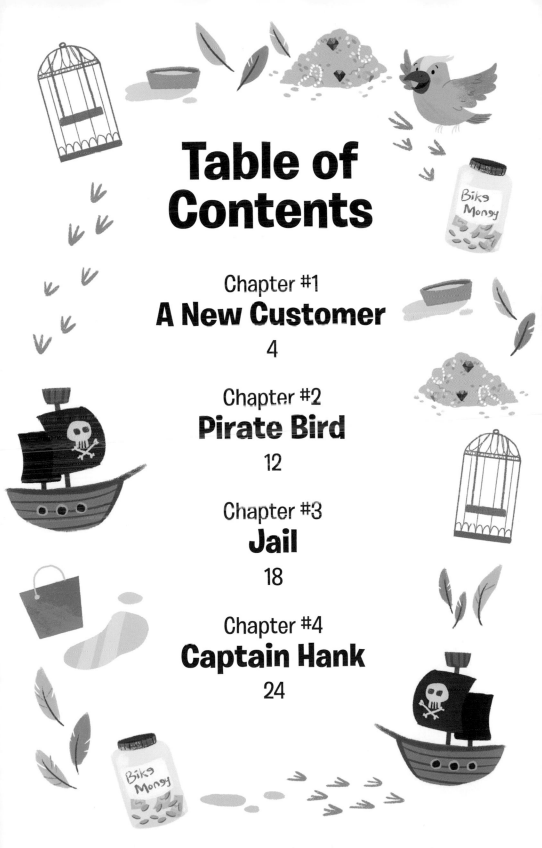

Table of Contents

Chapter #1
A New Customer

It was summer. Hank's bike was still bent. He needed more money to buy a new one. His pet-sitting business was quiet.

"Janie loves you, Janie loves you," said a voice in Hank's ear.

Was Hank asleep? Maybe he was having a nightmare.

"Sorry," said Janie. "He doesn't usually get out of his cage."

Hank sat up. "What?"

Janie stood in his living room. Her bird dug into Hank's shoulder. If it weren't Janie's, this green bird would be kind of cool.

"Tsk," said Janie. "Don't scare him."

"Me? Don't scare HIM?" said Hank.

"Can you watch Pete for the weekend?" asked Janie. "We're going to visit my cousins. They're not good with animals. Last time my aunt let them get a cat, it looked more like a rat within a week."

"Like a rat," said Pete. "Like a rat."

"Sure," said Hank. Pete perched on Hank's shoulder.

"You should put flyers up," said Janie.

"JANIE should keep her NOSE out of other people's BUSINESS!" said Hank.

"Janie knows business!" said Pete.

"Oh, no," Hank and Janie said together.

"Pete likes treats," said Janie. "And scratches around his beak. And on his neck." She demonstrated. "Don't you, Pete?"

Pete stretched his neck. "Janie knows business, Janie knows business."

"Here's his mirror," said Janie. She slid it from her purse and looked at herself. She winked at her reflection and Hank rolled his eyes.

Janie didn't notice. "Pete loves to look at himself."

"Hmph," said Hank. "If he were a respectable parrot, he'd tell you to walk the plank." Hank scratched Pete's neck.

"Walk the plank, walk the plank," said Pete.

Hank grinned.

"Maybe you shouldn't talk this weekend," said Janie.

"Maybe you should go back home," said Hank.

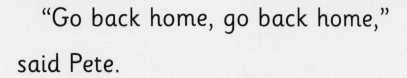

"Go back home, go back home,"
said Pete.

"Tsk," said Janie, leaving.

"Tsk, tsk," said Pete.

This was going to be a
weird weekend.

Chapter #2
Pirate Bird

When Janie was gone, Hank put Pete back on his shoulder and pretended he was a pirate.

"I'm Captain HANK!" he said. "Shiver me timbers! Swab the deck! Walk the plank!"

Pete cocked his head. "Pretty bird."

"Do you want your mirror?" Hank got it from Pete's cage then gave him a scratch.

Pete flew onto Hank's head. "Ow!"

Hank took Pete from his head and let him fly around the house instead.

"Hank!" called his mom. "Why is there a bird pooping on my kitchen floor?"

Uh-oh. Hank ran in for Pete. "Sorry, Mom. It's Janie's fault."

"Janie's fault, Janie's fault," said Pete as Hank put him back on his shoulder.

"Put him in his cage, Hank," said his mom.

"That's too much like jail!" Hank said. "Besides, I want to teach him how to be a real pirate bird! Shiver me timbers! Swab the deck!"

"Swab the deck. Swab the deck," repeated Pete.

"What a good idea." Hank's mom handed him a mop. "Start swabbing, matey."

"Matey?" Hank said. "I'm Captain HANK!"

"Start swabbing, Captain Hank," his mom said.

Pete flew, talked pirate, and pooped all afternoon. Hank swabbed a LOT of decks. He was pooped.

Chapter #3
Jail

"Find the gold, Pete. Find the gold!" Hank said.

Pete flew out Hank's bedroom door and down the stairs. Oh no! Hank ran after Pete.

Hank heard his mom scream.

"Haaank!"

"Find the gold, find the gold," Pete said.

Pete had one of her earrings.

Hank's mom insisted Pete go to jail.

Hank put Pete in his cage.

Hank considered. Pete was a very smart bird. "Okay, I'll break you out of jail, but you have to promise: No more pooping. And no more looking for gold. Deal?"

Pete was busy drinking water.

Hank tried again. "Deal?"

"Deal?" Pete said.

It was good enough for Hank. He closed his bedroom door and opened the cage.

Pete flew out and landed right on Hank's shoulder. Like a real pirate bird!

"You know . . . " Hank said. "A real pirate would have a trick ready when Janie comes to pick you up."

"Maybe I should teach you a trick," Hank told Pete. He demonstrated a somersault.

"Walk the plank, find the gold," said Pete.

Hank used treats and finally got Pete to do a somersault.

"Wow!" said Hank. "Smart bird!"

He showed Pete his reflection. Pete pooped.

"Swab the deck," said Pete.

"Smart bird," said Hank.

"Smart bird!" repeated Pete.

Chapter #4
Captain Hank

"Go on, Pete," Hank said.

Janie was back, but Pete wouldn't do a somersault.

"What did you teach him?" Janie asked.

"Give me a second." Hank carried Pete into the dining room.

"Remember?" Hank asked Pete. He held a treat in his fingers. Pete cocked his head and looked at him.

"Deal?" Hank said.

"Deal?" Pete said back.

Hank carried Pete back in. "Okay, we're ready."

Janie pulled a bird treat out of her purse but Hank stopped her. "Don't distract him."

"I'm not. Mind your own business."

Hank looked at Pete and whispered, *"Now!"*

Pete ate the treat.

Pete drank some water.

Pete did not do a somersault.

Finally, Janie said it was time for them to go home.

Hank was crushed. He watched them walk across the lawn.

"Wait!" Hank ran over and scratched Pete on the neck. Maybe this would do it. *"Now, Pete. Now."*

PetSitting
ALL KinDS
Honk

Pete cocked his head. "Captain HANK is the best pirate and he knows business! Pete LOVES being here and being a pirate bird! Go home JANIE and walk the plank!"

"Yes!" said Hank.

"Hank loves Janie," said Pete.

Hank's face turned bright red.

Janie crossed her arms. "You taught my bird to say that?"

"No!" Hank scratched Pete's neck some more. "Come on, Pete! Captain HANK is the best . . ."

"Tsk," said Pete. "Hank loves Janie!"

Janie laughed as she paid Hank. He could hear her laughing all the way home. He could hear her laughing from next door.

Hank was ready for a new pet. And definitely ready for a new customer!